Puss in Boots

A PARRAGON BOOK

Published by
Parragon Books,
Unit 13–17, Avonbridge Trading Estate,
Atlantic Road, Avonmouth, Bristol BS11 9QD

Produced by
The Templar Company plc,
Pippbrook Mill, London Road, Dorking, Surrey RH4 1JE

Designed by Mark Kingsley-Monks

Printed and bound in Italy

ISBN 0-75250-763-X

Puss in
Boots

Retold by Caroline Repchuk
Illustrated by David Anstey

|| •PARRAGON• ||

There was once an old miller who died, and left a will dividing his property between his three sons. He gave his eldest son his mill, his second son his donkey, and his youngest son his cat.

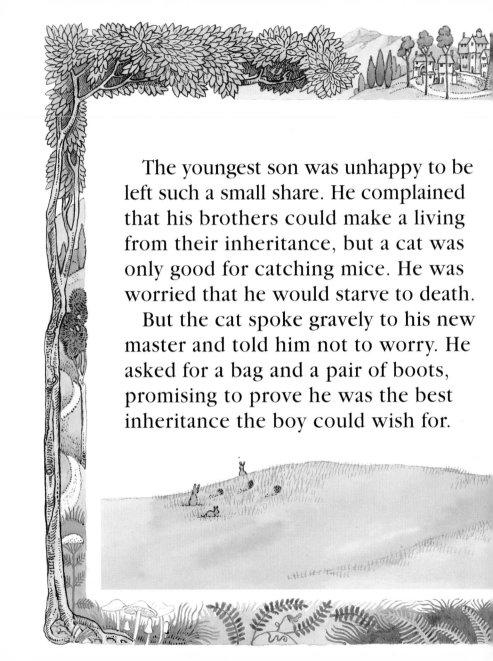

The youngest son was unhappy to be left such a small share. He complained that his brothers could make a living from their inheritance, but a cat was only good for catching mice. He was worried that he would starve to death.

But the cat spoke gravely to his new master and told him not to worry. He asked for a bag and a pair of boots, promising to prove he was the best inheritance the boy could wish for.

The youngest son decided to give the cat a chance, and with the last of his money bought a bag, a hat and a smart new pair of boots for the cat.

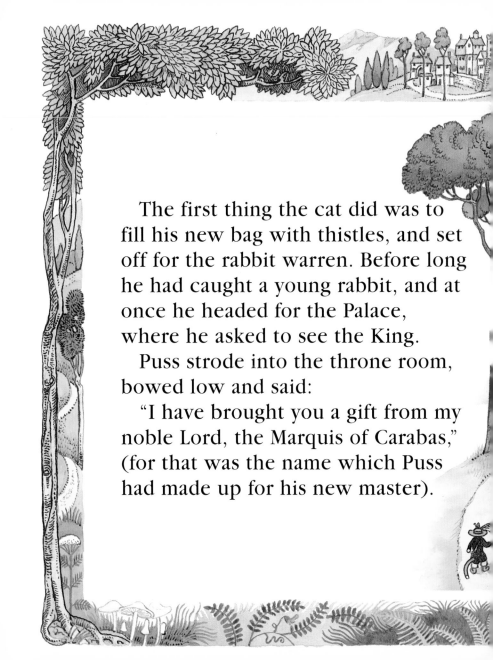

The first thing the cat did was to fill his new bag with thistles, and set off for the rabbit warren. Before long he had caught a young rabbit, and at once he headed for the Palace, where he asked to see the King.

Puss strode into the throne room, bowed low and said:

"I have brought you a gift from my noble Lord, the Marquis of Carabas," (for that was the name which Puss had made up for his new master).

"We hope your Royal Majesty will enjoy it."

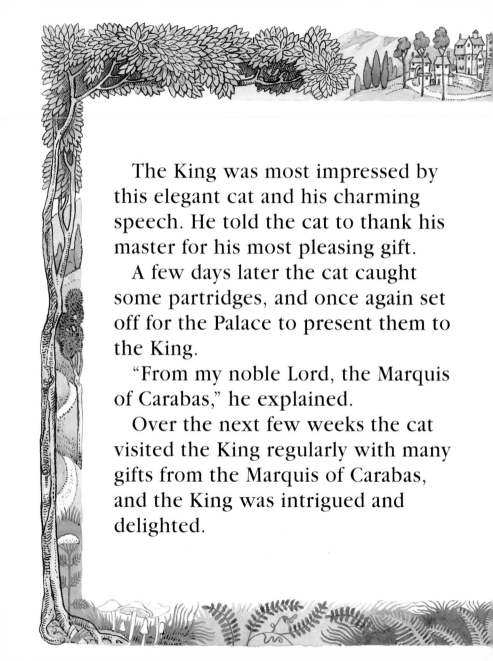

The King was most impressed by this elegant cat and his charming speech. He told the cat to thank his master for his most pleasing gift.

A few days later the cat caught some partridges, and once again set off for the Palace to present them to the King.

"From my noble Lord, the Marquis of Carabas," he explained.

Over the next few weeks the cat visited the King regularly with many gifts from the Marquis of Carabas, and the King was intrigued and delighted.

One day Puss heard that the King was to take a drive by the river with his beautiful daughter, the Princess.

The clever cat hurried to his master and told him, "Do as I say and your fortune will be made."

The young man went to the river, as the cat had told him, and after undressing, got in to bathe.

Soon the King passed by in his coach, and Puss began to cry out: "Help! My Lord Marquis of Carabas is drowning!"

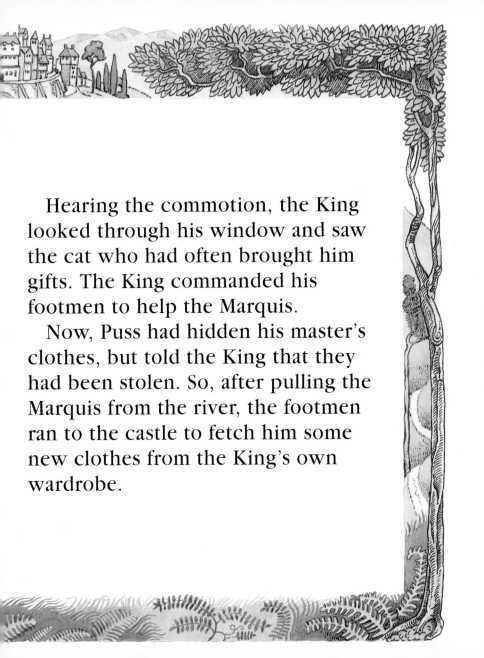

Hearing the commotion, the King looked through his window and saw the cat who had often brought him gifts. The King commanded his footmen to help the Marquis.

Now, Puss had hidden his master's clothes, but told the King that they had been stolen. So, after pulling the Marquis from the river, the footmen ran to the castle to fetch him some new clothes from the King's own wardrobe.

And so it was that clever Puss made sure his master met the beautiful Princess looking very fine and impressive indeed.

The Princess thought the young man was the most handsome she had ever seen, and he was just as taken with her.

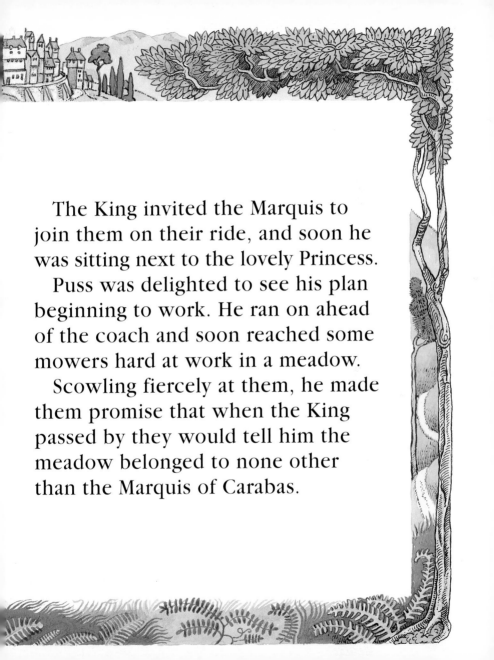

The King invited the Marquis to join them on their ride, and soon he was sitting next to the lovely Princess.

Puss was delighted to see his plan beginning to work. He ran on ahead of the coach and soon reached some mowers hard at work in a meadow.

Scowling fiercely at them, he made them promise that when the King passed by they would tell him the meadow belonged to none other than the Marquis of Carabas.

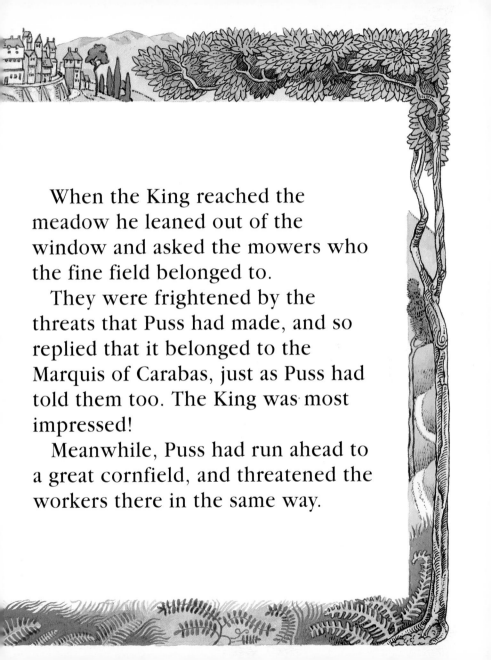

When the King reached the meadow he leaned out of the window and asked the mowers who the fine field belonged to.

They were frightened by the threats that Puss had made, and so replied that it belonged to the Marquis of Carabas, just as Puss had told them too. The King was most impressed!

Meanwhile, Puss had run ahead to a great cornfield, and threatened the workers there in the same way.

When the King arrived at the cornfield, he was again told that it belonged to the Marquis of Carabas. Most impressed, he congratulated him once more.

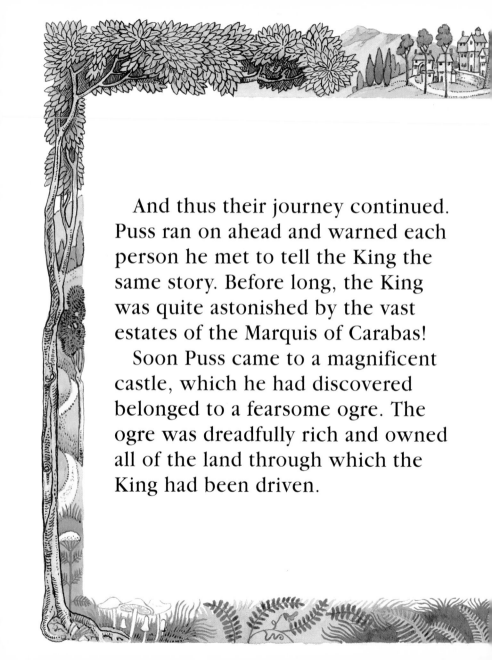

And thus their journey continued. Puss ran on ahead and warned each person he met to tell the King the same story. Before long, the King was quite astonished by the vast estates of the Marquis of Carabas!

Soon Puss came to a magnificent castle, which he had discovered belonged to a fearsome ogre. The ogre was dreadfully rich and owned all of the land through which the King had been driven.

Fearlessly, Puss strode up to the castle door and knocked loudly. The ogre was most surprised by his visitor, but Puss soon charmed him with flattering words, and the ogre invited him inside.

"I have heard," said Puss, "that you have magic powers. I have been told that you can change yourself into any creature you want. Is it true?"

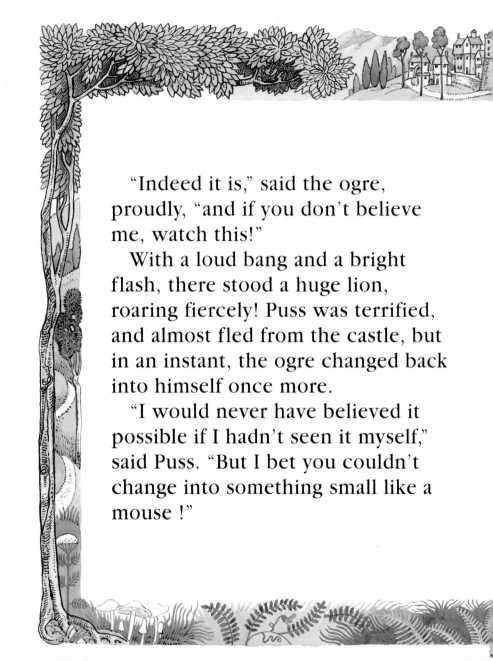

"Indeed it is," said the ogre, proudly, "and if you don't believe me, watch this!"

With a loud bang and a bright flash, there stood a huge lion, roaring fiercely! Puss was terrified, and almost fled from the castle, but in an instant, the ogre changed back into himself once more.

"I would never have believed it possible if I hadn't seen it myself," said Puss. "But I bet you couldn't change into something small like a mouse !"

"Oh, couldn't I?" said the ogre, feeling insulted. "Just watch this!"

With a flash and a bang he changed into a mouse and began to run about the floor.

In an instant, Puss pounced on him and gobbled him up in one bite!

And so, with the ogre gone for good, Puss had won a castle, lands and vast riches for his master.

Just then Puss heard the King's coach passing by so he ran out and bade the driver enter through the castle gates.

"Your Majesty is most welcome to the home of my lord Marquis of Carabas," said Puss, bowing low.

The King was astonished, and eagerly followed Puss inside with the Marquis and the Princess.

In the main hall a splendid banquet was waiting for them (for the ogre had liked to eat well!)

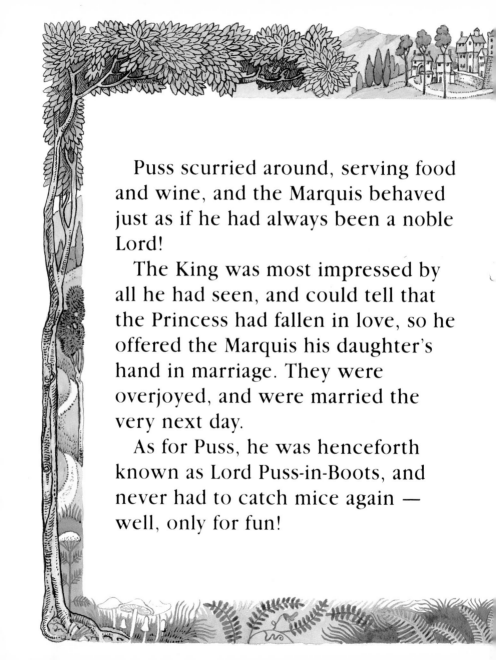

Puss scurried around, serving food and wine, and the Marquis behaved just as if he had always been a noble Lord!

The King was most impressed by all he had seen, and could tell that the Princess had fallen in love, so he offered the Marquis his daughter's hand in marriage. They were overjoyed, and were married the very next day.

As for Puss, he was henceforth known as Lord Puss-in-Boots, and never had to catch mice again — well, only for fun!

CHARLES PERRAULT

Puss in Boots first appeared in print in 1697 in the collection of fairy stories written by the French poet and storyteller, Charles Perrault (1628-1703).
The collection brought together many half-forgotten traditional folk tales, including *Bluebeard*, *Little Red Riding-Hood* and *Cinderella* and together they became known as *Mother Goose's Tales*. Written in a simple, unaffected style, Perrault's stories quickly became popular in France and later throughout the world. There has been considerable dispute over the years as to the exact author of these tales and some experts believe that it was actually Perrault's son, Pierre (1678-1700) who compiled and recorded the stories for posterity when he was only 17 or 18 years old.